A Horse's Best Friend

A KONA STORY

By Sibley Miller

Illustrated by Tara Larsen Chang and Jo Gershman

Feiwel and Friends

For Tali—Sibley Miller

To Mom and Dad—for all of your parenting and
nurturing instincts—Tara Larsen Chang

For my mom, who still always knows how
to make things better—Jo Gershman

A FEIWEL AND FRIENDS BOOK
An Imprint of Macmillan

Library of Congress Cataloging-in-Publication Data

Miller, Sibley.
A horse's best friend : a Kona story / by Sibley Miller ; illustrated by
Tara Larsen Chang and Jo Gershman. — 1st ed.
p. cm. — (Wind Dancers ; #9)
Summary: The tiny magical horses known as Wind Dancers all want to
keep the little puppy that shows up one day in the dandelion meadow,
but taking care of him is not as easy as they expect.
ISBN: 978-0-312-60542-1 (alk. paper)
[1. Horses—Fiction. 2. Dogs—Fiction. 3. Animals—Infancy—Fiction.
4. Magic—Fiction.]
I. Chang, Tara Larsen, ill. II. Gershman, Jo, ill. III. Title.
PZ7.M63373Hot 2011   [Fic]—dc22
2010014913

Series editor: Susan Bishansky
Designed by Barbara Grzeslo
Feiwel and Friends logo designed by Filomena Tuosto

First Edition: 2011

1 3 5 7 9 10 8 6 4 2

www.feiwelandfriends.com

CONTENTS

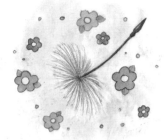

Meet the Wind Dancers

One day, a lonely little girl named Leanna blows on a doozy of a dandelion. To her delight and surprise, four tiny horses spring from the puff of the dandelion seeds!

Four tiny horses with shiny manes and shimmery wings. Four magical horses who can fly!

Dancing on the wind, surrounded by magic halos, they are the Wind Dancers.

The leader of the quartet is **Kona**. She has a violet-black coat and vivid purple mane, and she flies inside a halo of magical flowers.

Brisa is as pretty as a tropical sunset with her coral-pink color and blonde mane and tail.

Magical jewels make up Brisa's halo, and she likes to admire her gems (and herself) every time she looks in a mirror.

Sumatra is silvery blue with sea-green wings. Much like the ocean, she can shift from calm to stormy in a hurry! Her magical halo is made up of ribbons, which flutter and dance as she flies.

The fourth Wind Dancer is—surprise!—a colt. His name is Sirocco. He's a fiery gold, and he likes to go-go-go. Everywhere he goes, his magical halo of butterflies goes, too.

The tiny flying horses live together in the dandelion meadow in a lovely house carved out of the trunk of an apple tree. Every day, Leanna wishes she'll see the magical little horses again. (She's sure they're nearby, but she doesn't know they're invisible to people.) And the Wind Dancers get ready for their next adventure.

CHAPTER 1
Puppy Love

"Heads up, Brisa!" Kona called to her fellow Wind Dancer. "*Catch!*"

The tiny winged horses were flying above their dandelion meadow. Kona, the violet-colored leader of the group, was holding a bright red Jolly Ball between her front hooves. Coral-pink Brisa was bobbing with her head in the clouds.

"*Tra, la, la,*" Brisa warbled, poking at a low-flying cloud.

"Brisa!" Kona called again. "Come *on!*"

"Why don't you throw the ball to me

7

instead?" called Sirocco, the lone colt in the Wind Dancer foursome.

"Can't," Kona said. "We're playing ABC ball!"

"ABC ball?" piped up Sumatra. She was fluttering nearby, her halo of magic ribbons waving around her. "What's that?"

"We throw the ball to each other in alphabetical order, *of course*," Kona said. "Brisa goes first. She  throws the ball to me, because *K* for Kona comes after *B* for Brisa. Then I'll throw the ball to Sirocco. And Sumatra . . ."

Kona blinked at the sea-green filly.

". . . *you* get the ball last!"

"But what if I want to be first?" Sumatra

asked with a challenging nicker.

"You can't be first," Kona said primly. "SU-matra comes after SI-rocco. That's just the way it is!"

"Yeah, in *your* world, Miss Bossyhooves," Sumatra teased.

"Hey," Kona protested. "I am—"

"*—not bossy!*"

Brisa and Sirocco had jumped in together to finish Kona's sentence. Then they dissolved into giggles.

"Hey!" Kona said again. She looked hurt,  until Brisa swooped down to give her a nose nuzzle.

"Oh, don't feel bad," Brisa said. "We love you even if you *are* bossy!"

"And even if I don't necessarily *want* to

play ABC ball," Sumatra added with a mischievous grin.

"And even," Sirocco chimed in with his own sneaky smile, "if you *totally* think you're the mom of us."

"Oh, I do *not*!" Kona sputtered. And she was just about to go on about how *not* bossy or mom-like she was when she heard something that stopped her.

It was a rustling, scampering sound.

Which was followed by a *yap-yap-yapping* sound.

And *then* by a round, furry critter bursting out of a thick clump of yellow dandelions.

"*Arf, arf, ARF. Arf, arf, ARF!*"

The creature gazed up at the Wind Dancers with

bright, brown eyes. He reared up on his hind legs and waved his front paws. Then he lost his balance, fell over in a heap, and *arfed* some more.

"Oh!" Kona exclaimed. "Look! It's a *dog*!"

Her friends were just as enchanted as she was.

"Look at his shiny black-and-white coat!" Brisa cried. "And those sweet, floppy ears. And that adorable stubby tail!"

"Oh, I just *love* dogs," Sumatra said.

"Well, of course!" Sirocco agreed. "We *all* do. Dogs and horses go together perfectly. Like apples and honey. Or honey and oats. Or oatmeal and applesauce. Or—"

"Okay, we get the idea!" Sumatra said with a laugh.

"Come to think of it," she added, "every farm around here has a dog or two. Our big horse friends live with a Jack Russell terrier.

And there's a border collie in Leanna's barn."

"Lucky *them*!" Kona said enviously. Then she swooped to the ground, put her Jolly Ball on the grass, and hovered in front of the panting little ball of fur.

"Hello there!" she said. "I'm Kona. What's your name?"

The dog merely wagged his tail and gave Kona's face a very sloppy lick.

Puzzled, but still polite, Kona pointed her wet nose toward her friends.

"That's Sumatra, and Brisa," she told their new friend. "And that gold colt doing loop-de-loops is Sirocco."

Halfway through a loop-de-loop—and still upside down—Sirocco grinned at the dog.

"I'm always glad to meet another boy," he joked. "As you can see, I'm *surrounded* by fillies!"

"Well *someone* has to stay right side up around here," Sumatra said, rolling her eyes.

Kona turned her attention back to the black-and-white dog.

"And you are . . . ?" she asked. The flowers in her magical halo perked up expectantly.

"*Arf, arf, ARF!*" the dog replied. He

wagged his tail so hard that he flipped over onto his back.

"Ooh," Brisa realized, taking in the dog's baby-soft fur. "I know why he isn't talking to us! He's only a *puppy*!"

Suddenly, that puppy snatched up Kona's Jolly Ball in his pointy white  teeth, scampered several feet away, then tossed the ball to Sirocco.

Whinnying with delight, Sirocco caught the ball in *his* teeth and tossed it back to the puppy.

"He may not talk, but he sure knows how to play!" Sirocco announced happily.

This time, the puppy tossed the Jolly Ball to Brisa, who threw it to Sumatra, who zinged it back to the puppy. Kona so enjoyed watching the little dog running around with the horses' Jolly Ball that she didn't even mind that nobody was throwing the ball in alphabetical order!

Many bounces, tosses, and happy *arfs* later, horses and dog all collapsed among the dandelions, hot, tired, and happy.

After a brief rest, Kona flew over to the panting puppy and stroked the back of his head with her nose.

"There's a good boy," she cooed to him. "You're so cute! But . . ."

Suddenly Kona noticed something on the puppy's neck. Or rather, she noticed something *missing* from his neck.

"Don't dogs wear collars?" she asked her friends.

"Yup," Brisa answered. "Dogs have leather straps with jingly-jangly tags hanging from them. They're not nearly as pretty as *my* jeweled necklace, but they're still nice!"

"I don't think the collars are meant to be pretty," Kona pointed out. "The tags tell you who the dog belongs to in case it ever gets lost."

"Lost . . . like *our* puppy!" Brisa suddenly realized with wide eyes.

"What?" Sirocco scoffed. He flew over to pet the puppy reassuringly. "He's not lost. He's right here with us!"

Sumatra lifted her head from the fluffy

dandelion on which she'd been resting. Her green eyes looked troubled.

"No," she said, "Brisa's right. Maybe this puppy wandered away from his mother."

Kona felt like she could stroke the puppy's silky little head forever, but she knew she had to tear herself away to think about this. She fluttered high into the air above the other Wind Dancers.

"Maybe we can figure out where our puppy wandered off from."

Kona gazed across the meadow.

"From here, we're closest to the big horses' paddock," she reminded them. "Next is Leanna's farmhouse. And beyond that is town."

"Leanna's dog is a border collie, and she's black and white, just like this puppy," Sumatra said with confidence.

"Sure, but everything else is different!" Kona added, feeling a surge of joy. "Leanna's

border collie is long-legged and fluffy with a big, brushy tail. This little guy has short, sleek hair and a stumpy little tail. And he's pretty squat. No, Leanna's dog is definitely *not* our puppy's mother!"

"She sure isn't," Brisa quickly added with a laugh. "She's not even a she, the dog's a *he*!"

"Well that settles *that*," Kona replied with happiness.

"The big horses' Jack Russell terrier is brown and white," Sirocco added. "*She* sure isn't our dog's mother!"

"So our puppy must have wandered away from somebody's house in town," Sumatra decided. "But there are bunches of homes there! How will we ever find the one this pup came from?"

Kona landed on the grass in front of the puppy and gazed into his brown eyes. He gave her another wet lick, then wiggled happily when she rubbed his chin with her nose.

"We don't need to find his home," Kona suddenly declared.

"What do you mean?" Sumatra said.

Kona felt a zing in her belly.

"I mean," she told her three friends, "I think *we* should take care of this puppy! We'll adopt him! People do it all the time!"

"But we're not people," Brisa reminded her. "We're magic horses!"

"Even better," Kona said with a shrug. "Like Sirocco said, horses and dogs are made for each other!"

"You *do* have a point," Sumatra said.

"And it *would* be fun to have another boy in the family," Sirocco added.

"And he is sooooo cute," Brisa chimed in.

Kona clopped her hooves together in excitement. Then she looked seriously at her fellow horses.

"Taking care of a puppy is a really big responsibility," she told them. "Our puppy will need to be fed and walked and bathed . . ."

"Watch out," Brisa said to Sumatra and Sirocco with a giggle. "Kona's got somebody *else* to mother now!"

"That means less bossiness for us!" Sirocco replied with a sly grin.

But Kona wasn't listening to the others. She had fluttered happily into the air.

"C'mon, boy," the violet horse ordered the puppy sweetly. "Follow us! We're all going— *home*!"

CHAPTER 2
Barking up the Apple Tree

Going home was easier said than done.

The magical horses always winged themselves into their house high up the trunk of the apple tree. But the puppy could only scrabble at the tree's roots.

"I can't believe we didn't think of this!" Sumatra whinnied. "Dogs can't fly! How are we going to get him inside?"

"Easy," Kona said proudly. "We'll carry our puppy the way every doggy mama does."

"Huh?" Sirocco said, looking confused.

Kona nodded at her friends, then hovered

behind the puppy's head. Opening her mouth, she delicately nipped a fold of skin at the back of the dog's neck. Then she motioned the other Wind Dancers over with her tail.

Brisa, Sirocco, and Sumatra propped the dog up from underneath his front and back legs. Then—with the help of a little extra magic—the four horses lifted him off the ground and zipped him up to their tree house.

The dog *just* fit into the living room.

"*Whoa!*" Sumatra laughed as the puppy's wagging tail bonked her in the nose. "It's a little *crowded* in here."

"Oh, don't listen to her," Sirocco assured their furry guest. "Sumatra likes everything *just* so. But take it from me—I make messes in our house *all* the time!"

"And he means *all* the time!" Sumatra agreed with a roll of her green eyes.

"He's just lucky he has *me* to pretty up the

place afterward," Brisa told the puppy. She popped a magic jewel out of her halo and onto the living-room wall to demonstrate.

Meanwhile, Kona just stared at the puppy as he sniffed around his new home, his cute black nose twitching and his tail *thump-thump-thumping* against the walls.

"That's it," Kona encouraged him. "Explore, explore!"

She turned to the other horses and explained, "Sniffing is how dogs get to know new surroundings."

"We know that," Sumatra replied. "After all, it's what *horses* do, too."

But the Wind Dancers had never sniffed quite like this!

The puppy was snuffling so hard that he sucked one of Kona's flowery

throw rugs right off the floor! Then he sniffed one of Sumatra's ribbon window curtains and pulled that down, too.

Next the dog bounded into the kitchen and began gnawing on the wooden table.

"No, puppy! No, no, no!" Sumatra neighed, clopping after him.

The dog responded by wagging his tail so hard, he accidentally knocked Sumatra over!

"Ooh!" Sumatra cried in surprise.

Brisa tried to suppress a giggle as she told Sumatra, "At least he *listened* to you!"

She was right. The puppy had left the table behind and moved on . . . to one of the jewel mirrors Brisa had placed on the tree house's walls!

"No, puppy! No, no, no!" Brisa cried.

This time it was Sumatra who giggled as Brisa cantered over to rescue her mirror.

But none of the Wind Dancers laughed at what happened next.

"Uh, what's that?" Sirocco asked nervously. He was pointing with his front hoof at the floor beneath the puppy's paws.

Or rather, at the *puddle* forming on the floor beneath the puppy's paws.

"No, puppy!" the horses neighed together. "No, no, no!"

"I think," Kona said, dashing over to grab

25

the scruff of the puppy's neck, "that our puppy is going to be an *outdoor* dog!"

"You can say *that* again!" Sirocco said, rushing to help Kona hoist up their new pet. Sumatra and Brisa quickly joined them. As swiftly—and as magically—as they'd flown the puppy up to the tree house, they had him down on the ground again.

For the first time since the horses had met him, the puppy's stumpy tail stopped wagging. He even whimpered ever so slightly.

Kona rushed to pet him.

"Don't be sad," she cooed, giving the dog a nose nuzzle. "You didn't mean to do it, right Baxter?"

The other Wind Dancers gaped at each other for a moment.

"Baxter?" Brisa squeaked. "How did the puppy become *Baxter*?"

"Everybody needs a name!" Kona said.

"So *you* decided on his?" Sirocco asked.

"It's a mother's job to come up with a name for her . . . puppy," Kona sniffed.

"See!" Sumatra said. "You *do* want to be the mom of everybody."

"Not *everybody*," Kona retorted. Then she ducked her head and muttered, "Just . . . this puppy."

"Come on, Kona," Sirocco said. "He's *our* puppy, right? We should figure out his name *together*."

"Well, what do *you* suggest, smarty-colt?" Kona asked with an eye roll.

"A *boy* dog needs a *cool* name—like Sirocco!" Sirocco declared.

"Or a beautiful name, like Brisa!" the coral filly piped up.

"How about a *windy* name," Sumatra suggested. "To go with our Wind Dancery ones."

"But how do we find one?" Brisa wondered. "Our names just came to us the day Leanna blew us out of the dandelion."

"So, let's do the same thing we did that day," Kona declared.

"Okay," Sirocco said. "That means we'll close our eyes and shout out the first words that occur to us."

"Yes, exactly," Kona said approvingly. "Ready?"

"Yup!" Sirocco said, squeezing his eyes shut.

"Me, too!" Brisa said, fluttering her blonde lashes closed.

"Me, three!" Sumatra added, shutting her eyes as well.

After a moment of quiet, Sirocco piped up.

"Got it!" he shouted. "Pudding!"

"Si-ROCCO," Kona scolded. "That's not a name!"

"What?" Sirocco protested. "It's the first thing I thought of. I must be hungry."

"You're *always* hungry," Kona said with a smile. "That's no excuse. Try again."

"How about . . . Bow-tie?" Sumatra said,  looping one of her magical blue ribbons into a pretty bow as she said it.

"Beauty!" Brisa offered.

"*Carrot* pudding?" Sirocco whinnied.

Kona stared at her friends.

"Wrong, wrong, and wrong!" she neighed. "Baxter's better than all of those."

She closed her eyes again and pictured her plump little puppy bounding through the dandelion meadow. She imagined him leaping after the Jolly Ball. She saw his silky ears blowing in the breeze.

"*Zephyr!*" Kona finally blurted.

Her eyes popped open, and she said the name again.

"Zephyr!"

The adorable puppy panted and wagged his tail in approval.

The other Wind Dancers grinned, too!

"It's pretty!" Brisa voted.

"And windy," Sumatra agreed.

"And boyish!" Sirocco whinnied.

Kona smiled as the puppy—Zephyr—bounded over to her and gave her a big, wet kiss.

"It's the *perfect* name," she proudly said. And then, just to herself because she didn't want Brisa, Sumatra, and Sirocco to call her a bossyhooves again, she added: *And I gave it to Zephyr, just like a mama should!*

CHAPTER 3

Early to Bed,
Early to Rise

At dinner at the bottom of the tree that night, Kona proudly presented Zephyr with a plate of steamed parsnips.

He sniffed at the fragrant veggies.

"*Arf?*" he barked curiously.

"Try them," Sirocco encouraged the puppy. "They're great. See?"

The colt nibbled at the parsnips for Zephyr's benefit. When the puppy didn't immediately follow suit, Sirocco took another, slightly bigger bite. And another, and another—

"Si-RO-cco!" Kona neighed. "That's Zephyr's dinner!"

"Well, maybe our puppy just doesn't like parsnips," Sumatra said between bites of the oat cake she was eating. "Because Zephyr doesn't seem to be eating his."

"Maybe he'd prefer an oat cake," Kona said. With her teeth, she swiped away Sumatra's food and plopped it in front of the puppy.

"Hey!" Sumatra complained.

But Kona didn't seem to hear her. She was smiling at Zephyr, encouraging him to eat.

The puppy pounced on the oat cake with a happy yip! But after gnawing away on it for a moment, he left the other (slobbery, chewed-on) half untouched.

Kona shrugged and returned the oat cake to Sumatra.

"I guess he's not that hungry," Kona said.

"Now I'm not either!" Sumatra said, sticking her tongue out at the slimy oat cake. Once again, Kona didn't seem to notice.

Sumatra tried to put the slight (and her hunger) out of her mind.

After all, she thought with a sweet gaze at the puppy, *it's not Zephyr's fault if Kona is a little . . . distracted.*

After dinner, the Wind Dancers snuggled with Zephyr in a bed of soft leaves under the tree. Each horse told Zephyr a bedtime story.

Sumatra wove a tale about a magic carpet of ribbons.

Brisa's story was all about a day of pampering at a beauty spa for horses, complete with carrot slices on her eyes and a mane-and-tail treatment!

And Sirocco read Zephyr his favorite recipe for Sirocco Surprise Cake.

Kona told the last story.

"Once upon a time, there were four magical horses, four *big* horses, and a Jolly Ball . . ." she began.

As she told Zephyr about the soccer game that the eight horses had played with that

Jolly Ball, she tied one of Sumatra's silky magic ribbons around the puppy's downy neck. She attached the other end of the ribbon to the trunk of the apple tree.

". . . and that," she said in a soothing voice, "is how the great soccer match was won! The End."

Zephyr panted contentedly, then sniffed curiously at his ribbon leash.

"That's to keep you nice and safe while you sleep in your cozy bed," Kona said, fluffing up Zephyr's leaf pile with her nose. "Nighty-night, now!"

She gave Zephyr a quick nose nuzzle, then whispered to the others, "Let's hit the hay."

Together, the Wind Dancers flew up to the apple tree house and clopped downstairs to their sleeping stalls.

"I think it's going all right," Sumatra

declared between big yawns, "having Zephyr live with us."

"It's going *better* than all right!" Sirocco whinnied. "Tomorrow I'm going to teach our boy puppy how to do backflips!"

"I bet Zephyr will be even more cute tomorrow than he was today," Brisa sighed.

"I *told* you he belongs here!" Kona said to her friends as they settled into their stalls. "I, I mean *we* are taking such good care of him."

Kona stretched and yawned.

"It's hard work, though," she admitted. "I'm beat."

The other Wind Dancers agreed. They fluffed the straw mats on the floors of their stalls, nestled beneath their ribbon-y horse blankets, and snuggled up with their sleep buddies. It was only a minute or two before each of the Wind Dancers began to fall sound asleep—

"Hooowwwwlllll!"

Sirocco awoke with a snort. So did the fillies.

"What a *dream* I just had," Sirocco said through a yawn. "There was a puppy in it. A very *loud* puppy . . ."

"Hooowwwwlllll!"

Kona burst out of her stall.

"That's no dream," she whinnied. "It's Zephyr! Let's go see what's wrong with him!"

By the time the Wind Dancers landed in a circle around Zephyr, he was howling his head off! But when the puppy saw them, his yowls turned into mere whimpers.

"I bet he's hungry!" Sirocco piped up. He zipped back up to their apple tree house and returned with a big, moist apple muffin.

But the sad puppy didn't touch it.

"I guess I'll just have to eat it myself, then," Sirocco said with a big shrug. As he gobbled up the muffin, Brisa cocked her head at their sleepless puppy.

"Maybe he just needs soothing," Brisa whispered to her friends.

She stroked Zephyr's nose and told him, "You're the most adorable puppy I ever saw. Why, you're almost as pretty as me!"

Zephyr looked at Brisa blankly, then whimpered some more.

"*I* think he's cold," Sumatra declared. She quickly wove up a pretty blanket of her magic ribbons and draped it over Zephyr's

back. But with one agitated shimmy, the puppy shook the blanket off.

Kona hesitated. Her friends were full of ideas about what to do for Zephyr—and she had none. Except for one thing!

"Come here, Zephyr," she said softly, cozying up to the puppy. "I'll stay with you until you fall asleep."

Zephyr immediately curled up against Kona and gave a shuddery sigh. His whimpers turned into drowsy snuffles.

Kona had (somehow) given Zephyr *just* what he wanted. She couldn't help but beam with triumph as she waved her friends away with her hoof.

"You all go on back to bed," she said. "I'll stay with Zephyr until he's asleep."

"Are you sure?" Brisa asked, even as she cast a longing, sleepy look up at the tree house.

"Of course!" Kona said. "It's a mama's job to comfort her young."

"Right," Sumatra agreed with a nod.

And Sumatra *did* agree. She wanted Zephyr to be happy. But at the same time, she realized, her voice sounded quite wistful.

Zephyr's getting the most of Kona, Sumatra found herself thinking. Then she shook her head in confusion.

Isn't that what we all want? she asked herself. *For Zephyr to be happy? And, for that matter, for Kona to be the* bossyhooves *of someone else, for a change?*

Sumatra nodded her head in answer to her own question. But deep down, she wondered if she *really* wanted to let go of Kona—bossyhooves and all!

After lots of cooing and petting, Zephyr finally drifted off to sleep. Kona grinned proudly.

What a feat! she thought, as she carefully pulled away from the puppy and fluttered up to the tree house door. *I was able to get Zephyr to sleep—*

"*Hooowwwwllllll!*"

"Oh, noooo!" Kona cringed. She glanced down to see Zephyr awake and looking up at her with the loneliest brown eyes she'd ever seen.

With a sigh, Kona rejoined the puppy on his leafy bed and soothed him to sleep *again*. But when she, once more, tried to slip away—

"Hooowwwwlllll!"

And that's how Kona spent the longest night of her life!

. . .

When Brisa, Sumatra, and Sirocco emerged from their tree house the next morning—bright-eyed and ready for the day's adventure— Kona was *still* outside with Zephyr and fast asleep!

"Good *morning?*" Sumatra neighed, landing on the ground next to Kona and the puppy. She was shocked! Kona was usually the first Wind Dancer up in the morning—getting breakfast ready for her three friends.

Zephyr, who'd been snoozing happily by Kona's side, popped up and *arfed* hello.

"Oooh!" Brisa cooed at the puppy. "You *are* even cuter than you were yesterday!"

But when she glanced at Kona, she gulped.

43

The violet-black filly was stumbling to her hooves. Leaves were tangled up in her mane, and her eyelashes were clumped and heavy.

"Oh, Kona!" Brisa whinnied, her eyes wide. "*Clearly* you didn't get much beauty sleep last night!"

"But she's still up in time to make us

breakfast!" Sirocco said cheerfully. He flew down and landed next to Kona. "So, what are we having?"

"Breakfast?" Kona said dully.

"You know," Sirocco prompted her. "Apple pancakes or apple muffins? I'd even be happy with a simple baked apple—with *lots* of cinnamon and sugar, of course."

"How about *just* apples," Kona muttered, pointing with her nose at their tree's rosy fruits.

"Just . . . apples? *Plain* apples?" Sirocco neighed. "Sure, that makes a yummy *snack*. But we're talking *breakfast* here. Breakfast needs to be cooked! I think that's a rule or something."

The butterflies in his magic halo agreed, sagging disappointedly.

Sumatra shook her head in bewilderment as she flew up to pluck an apple from a nearby branch.

"I wonder what *Zephyr's* going to get for *his* breakfast," she said. Once again she felt a pang in her belly.

But Kona didn't seem to notice. She only yawned and slumped back onto Zephyr's leafy bed. Meanwhile, the puppy bounded out into the dandelion meadow, then ran back to the horses, then dashed back into the meadow again.

"All that running back and forth means Zephyr wants to play," Kona said sleepily, her eyes closing.

"Well, *that's* not hard to figure out," Sumatra said through a noisy bite of apple. "Dogs *always* want to play!"

"So do horses!" Sirocco neighed through

his own bite of plain old apple.

"Well," Kona said sleepily, "have a go at it then. I'm just going to rest my eyes . . . for a minute. . . ."

Before the other Wind Dancers could protest, the violet horse had fallen back asleep!

CHAPTER 4
A Doggy Discovery

"We should be planning our day's adventure right now," Sumatra complained to Brisa and Sirocco, "instead of waiting for Kona to catch her Zs."

"*Arf, arf, ARF,*" Zephyr barked, jumping up on Sumatra and giving her a sloppy lick that also caught a good bit of her apple. Intrigued, the puppy took a nibble of Sumatra's breakfast—then spit it out.

"I guess you're not crazy about plain apples for breakfast either," Sumatra said to the puppy, sighing as she gently rubbed him

 48

behind the ears with her muzzle.

After a moment, Zephyr trotted away, sniffing at the ground.

"Maybe he's looking for a breakfast he finds more *tasty*," Sumatra muttered to herself. "In fact, maybe I should do that, too!"

She turned to invite Brisa and Sirocco along, but they were absorbed in a game of Bonk the Apple.

Or at least Sirocco was.

Bonk!

Sirocco head-butted his breakfast toward the pink filly and called, "C'mon, Brisa. Now you bonk it back to me!"

"Sirocco!" Brisa squeaked, letting the apple fall to the ground. "Don't bonk apples at me—you'll get my mane all juicy! I'm not going to bonk any to *you*, either. But, hmmm, I could use the apple *seeds* to buff up my hooves. They look a *tiny* bit dull."

"Bo-ring!" Sirocco argued as he bonked another apple at her.

Sumatra sighed.

"Looks like everyone's doing their own thing this morning," she said to herself. So she drifted off on an air current, wondering if some blackberries might make her belly feel less pangy.

When Sumatra arrived at some berry bushes near the big horses' paddock on the edge of the dandelion meadow, she plucked a big juicy berry and ate it.

She ate a few more berries. They were delicious—but they didn't exactly make her happy.

She didn't bother to pick some extra blackberries for Kona to cook with, either, as she usually would do.

Clearly, Kona's not in a cooking mood

today, she thought sadly. The ribbons in her magic halo went limp in agreement.

But as Sumatra flew over the big horses' paddock on her way back to the apple tree, she heard a familiar sound.

"Arf!"

The bark sounded just like Zephyr's, only louder and lower!

Sumatra paused in the air and looked down to see the big horses' Jack Russell terrier, Daisy. She was lying just inside the door of the barn next to the paddock. Her chin was plopped onto her front paws.

"She looks sort of sad, too," Sumatra noted, swooping down for a closer look. Sumatra wasn't the only one paying attention to Daisy.

 Thelma and Fluff, the mare and filly who lived in the paddock,  were nickering at the dog.

"*Arf! Arf!*" Daisy answered the horses.

Sumatra smiled.

"If I spoke *arf,* I'd bet you that Daisy was saying, 'Leave me alone!'"

But Thelma and Fluff *didn't* leave the pooch alone. Thelma gave Daisy's nose a lick, then Fluff nudged Daisy so forcefully that the Jack Russell *had* to get to her feet.

And once Daisy was up, Thelma began to playfully chase her. Despite herself, the dog began to trot. Then she started to run. And before long, Daisy was romping and leaping all over the paddock. She even dragged a green Jolly Ball out of the barn and nosed it to Thelma for a game of catch.

"Wow!" Sumatra whispered in awe. "Thelma and Fluff totally cheered that dog up! They're so big and strong, they sort of gave Daisy no choice. She *had* to get up and play with them."

As Sumatra continued to watch Daisy, Thelma, and Fluff play together, she was struck by how *easy* everything seemed to be. There was no hoisting Daisy into a high-up tree house (and no rushing her back out again when nature called!).

There was no coaxing her to eat horsey foods like apples and parsnips that she didn't seem to like.

Even the big horses' big size seemed more suited to doggy friendship.

There's no way we could horse-handle Zephyr into playing the way Thelma and Fluff just did with Daisy, Sumatra added to herself.

As she flew back to the dandelion meadow, all these thoughts made Sumatra's belly feel pangier than ever.

When Sumatra arrived back home, Kona was still snoozing beneath the apple tree, and Brisa and Sirocco were playing with Zephyr.

Or rather, Zephyr was *trying* to play with them!

"*Arf, arf, ARF!*"

Zephyr jumped up on his hind legs and waved his paws at the flying colt and the coral filly. He ran in circles, and as he did, he motioned at the horses with his nose.

"What's he up to?" Sirocco asked Brisa, his ears pricked forward inquisitively.

Brisa eyed the still-scampering puppy.

"Maybe he wants to dance!" the filly chirped. "Come on, Zephyr. I'll teach you some dressage moves. They're sooooo pretty!"

Brisa began to wave her front hooves

daintily and bob her head so her mane flowed
in the breeze.

"*Arf, arf, ARF!*"

Zephyr shook his head and continued to
run in circles.

"I don't think dressage is Zephyr's thing,"
Sirocco pointed out.

While Brisa and Sirocco bickered about beauty, Sumatra cocked her head and stared at Zephyr. Something about the puppy's motions looked familiar. . . .

"Hey, I know what Zephyr's doing!" she blurted suddenly.

Sirocco and Brisa jumped and looked over at her.

"Oh, you're back!" Brisa said, giving Sumatra a happy nuzzle.

"So, tell!" Sirocco demanded. "What's our dog up to?"

"He's trying to *herd* you!" Sumatra declared. "Remember when I met Sassafras, the cow-horse, out on the range? That circle-y thing is just what she did to round up her cattle."

"Herding, huh?" Sirocco said. "I forgot that some dogs are bred to herd sheep or cows."

Then he looked down at Zephyr and laughed.

"Sorry, buddy," he said to the puppy. "I guess it's kind of hard to herd a horse who can just fly out of your reach!"

Sirocco darted playfully above Zephyr's head, and nickered teasingly at the pup.

But if Sirocco expected Zephyr to giggle along with him, the colt was disappointed.

"*Arf, arf, ARF!*" Zephyr barked indignantly. He ran to the base of the apple tree and grabbed the Wind Dancers' Jolly Ball from its spot among the tree roots. Then Zephyr began to race across the meadow with the ball.

He wasn't scampering.

And he wasn't *arfing* playfully.

He was simply sprinting away!

Before anyone knew it, Zephyr and his Jolly Ball had disappeared into a tall thatch of weeds.

"Ooh," Brisa burbled. "Zephyr wants to play hide and seek!"

"Ready or not, here we come!" Sirocco

neighed loudly. So loudly, that Kona—who had still been snoring away under the apple tree—jolted awake.

"We're playing hide and seek with Zephyr," Brisa reported to Kona.

"Hide and seek?" Kona said, suddenly aloft. She scanned the meadow for a glimpse of Zephyr's bobbing tail or flopping ears. Seeing none, her eyes went wide.

"He's doing a pretty good job of hiding, isn't he?" she said to her friends, sounding a bit worried.

"*Relax*," Sirocco said. "Zephyr just zipped into that patch of weeds over there."

But as the Wind Dancers flew over to the weeds, Sumatra couldn't help but feel as uneasy as Kona did.

"Come out, come out wherever you are!" Brisa burbled.

The Wind Dancers waited for the weeds to

rustle, for the puppy to come tumbling out into the meadow and toss the Jolly Ball.

But he didn't.

"Come on, Zephyr!" Sirocco said playfully. He dove down into the weeds and thrashed around to root out the puppy.

But when he poked his golden head back out and looked up at Kona, Sumatra, and Brisa, this is what he said:

"He's not here. Zephyr's gone!"

CHAPTER 5
Hide and Seek
(the Puppy)

Kona felt panicky as the four horses fanned out across the meadow in search of the puppy.

"Zephyr," she called as loudly as she could. *"Ze-phyrrrrrr!"*

Not so much as a yap in response.

"Where could he be?" she asked her friends.

"I don't know!" Brisa cried. "And if a dog is a horse's best friend, *shouldn't* we know?"

I don't know where Zephyr went, but I think I know why he ran away from us, Sumatra thought to herself sadly. *As much as*

we love him, Zephyr doesn't belong with us!

But she didn't have the heart to tell her friends her thoughts while they were all so worried about their puppy.

Besides, Kona wouldn't have given her the chance. She was back in bossyhooves mode!

"We're going to search the woods," Kona ordered her wide-eyed friends. "There are lots of places for a puppy to hide there."

The Wind Dancers zipped over to the edge of the woods, searching for any sign of their black-and-white friend.

But they saw nothing.

 Then Kona spotted a flash of red. It was next to a tree trunk nearby.

"Let's see!" Kona said, zipping over to investigate. A moment later, she neighed.

The good news? The color Kona had seen was a scrap of red rubber. Kona was certain it was part of the Jolly Ball Zephyr had been carrying when he made his escape.

The bad news? There was still no sign of Zephyr!

But then Kona spotted *another* bit of red rubber in a nearby pond and zipped over to it.

As Kona arrived, with the other Wind Dancers on her tail, the rubber scrap rose out of the water like magic!

Kona gasped—until she saw that magic had nothing to do with the levitating Jolly Ball scrap. It was a frog! The rubber sat atop his head like a little cap.

"Oh, how stylish!" Brisa giggled.

Ribbit! The frog scowled. Clearly, he wasn't feeling fashionable!

"Whoops," the pink filly gulped. "Sorry, sorry!"

And the horses flew on.

They found a bit of red rubber in a nest full of squawking baby birds.

 A moment later, Kona spotted still another Jolly Ball scrap. This one was plugging up a mouse hole beneath a tree!

By then, the Wind Dancers had found so many rubber scraps, Kona couldn't imagine what was left of the Jolly Ball except—

"—the handle!" Kona cried, spotting the U-shaped tube of red rubber beneath a tree.

She swooped down to nip up the final Jolly Ball piece. Then she looked around hopefully for Zephyr.

She almost cried when she saw nothing. But before she could utter her first sob, she *heard* something off in the distance.

"*Arf, arf, ARF!*"

Kona perked up and pointed her nose toward the sound.

"I think that's Zephyr!" she said.

The Wind Dancers raced toward Zephyr's *arfs*. As they emerged from the woods, they saw their puppy bounding through the middle of the meadow.

"Zephyrrrrrr!" Kona neighed as loudly as she could.

The puppy stopped in his tracks!

Kona held her breath as her fluffy little pup looked back at her.

"Come here, boy!" Kona called.

Zephyr took a step or two in the Wind Dancers' direction.

"Yay!" Brisa whinnied.

But then Zephyr stopped and looked back over his shoulder.

"Boo!" Sirocco rumbled.

Kona saw Zephyr's floppy ears perk up.

"He hears something!" she said. "But what?"

"Well, you know dogs' ears are super-strong," Sumatra noted wisely. "It must be something we *can't* hear."

"And something intriguing, from the looks of it," Sirocco added.

"Maybe it's something *pretty*!" Brisa cooed.

 66

"Um, Brisa?" Sumatra said. "You can't *hear* beauty."

"Oh, I can!" Brisa said earnestly. Sirocco rolled his eyes and laughed.

But laughing was the last thing Kona felt like doing. She was too nervous about her, that is, *their* puppy.

"We have to follow Zephyr!"

Kona started flying after the swiftly departing puppy.

Sumatra felt yet another pang as she, Brisa, and Sirocco trailed the violet-black horse.

"Hey," Brisa called, "it looks like Zephyr's running to the horse paddock."

As the puppy reached the paddock at the edge of the meadow, he seemed to grow even more excited. His stumpy tail wagged so hard, it blurred, and his *arfs* were louder than ever.

"Wow, listen to Zephyr," Sirocco said. "He sounds like a *pack* of puppies!"

Kona cocked her head. Sirocco was right. Zephyr *was* making a whole lot of *arfs* for just one little dog.

As the group made its way toward the big open doors of the paddock's barn, the *arfs* grew even louder!

Then out of the barn scampered a crowd of five little dogs—all of whom looked *very* familiar! They had sleek black-and-white coats and squat legs. And as they scrambled into the hay-strewn dirt of the paddock, they wiggled their stumpy tails. They looked *exactly* like Zephyr!

"It *was* a pack of puppies!" Brisa cried. "Look at them all!"

Kona gaped.

"They are who Zephyr heard," she said, "long before we could."

Trotting with the pack of puppies were two full-grown dogs.

One was Daisy, the big horses' Jack Russell terrier!

The other was Leanna's black-and-white border collie, Hugo!

And just behind *him* was Leanna herself, holding her dog's leash.

Daisy barked. Hugo barked. And all five puppies barked, too. Then they pounced on Zephyr, showering him with welcoming licks and tail-wags.

Kona was stunned.

"So those are . . ." she said with a quaver in her voice.

"Zephyr's brothers and sisters!" Brisa said.

Kona's eyes widened in shock.

Sumatra snuggled up to Kona in the air.

"It looks like Zephyr got his black-and-white coloring from his border collie dad," she said, "and his short hair, tail, and legs . . . from his Jack Russell mom. We hadn't thought about that. But he's a mutt!"

"He's *their* mutt," Kona said, watching Zephyr yip with joy as he was reunited with his family.

"And not *just* theirs . . ." Sirocco said, pointing with his nose to the far side of the paddock. The big horses—Thelma, Benny, Fluff, and Andy—were peering over at the commotion. When they spied the missing puppy among the throng of dogs, they cantered over.

"Puppy number three!" Thelma neighed at Zephyr triumphantly. "You're back!"

"Oh . . ." Kona said, as her lower lip trembled. "I guess Zephyr's really home now, home where he belongs."

On cue, the Wind Dancers winged down to give Zephyr good-bye nose nuzzles.

Kona gave Zephyr the biggest nose nuzzle of all.

The puppy *arfed* happily at his little horsey friends, then went back to frolicking with his doggy family.

For the first time that day, Sumatra's belly felt pang-less.

But Kona felt only sad.

"My guess," Sumatra suggested gently to Kona, "is that Leanna and Hugo come to visit the puppies every day. *We* could visit Zephyr a lot, too."

"And if he's sleeping *here*," Brisa noted sweetly, "then *you* don't have to camp outside with Zephyr at our tree house. You'll get your beauty rest back!"

"I know you'll miss Zephyr," Sumatra added, "we all will, but *we've* missed *you, too*! Your nose nuzzles . . ."

"Your amazing cooking . . ." Sirocco said.

"Even your . . . bossiness!" Sumatra continued, with a sly grin.

Kona shook her head. "I am—"

"—*not bossy!*" Sumatra, Sirocco, and Brisa chorused. They grinned at Kona.

And despite the pangs in *her* belly, Kona couldn't help smiling back.

"Okay, fine," she agreed. "Maybe I *am* a bossyhooves sometimes. For instance, right now, I *order* you all to come over here!"

Sirocco, Sumatra, and Brisa fluttered close to the violet-black filly.

And *that's* when Kona gave her friends, all at once, a big, sweet—and most mom-like— nose nuzzle.

A Puppy by Another Name

The next afternoon, the Wind Dancers were back, perched on the paddock fence where the big horses (and dogs) lived. They grinned as they watched Zephyr frolic with his puppy siblings.

They weren't the only ones enjoying the puppy action. Doggy mom Daisy was eyeing the little pooches with maternal watchfulness. Leanna and Hugo were there, too. And so were the big horses.

"Now don't be too rough, Puppies 1, 2, 4, 5, and 6," Thelma admonished. "And Puppy 3, make sure you don't wander off again!"

Almost as if she could understand what

 74

the horses were saying, Leanna suddenly said to herself, "I think these puppies could really use some names. I wonder what we should call them."

Sumatra gasped.

"This is the perfect moment to give Leanna our present!" she exclaimed.

Kona smiled and nodded.

She looked down at the six ribbons looped around her neck. Then, giving her friends a nod, she launched off the fence and zipped over to the little doggy food bowls lined up against the barn wall.

She laid one of her presents in front of each bowl, then darted back to her friends.

Soon enough, Leanna ambled over to a bin near the fence. Using a scoop, she dug some brown pellets out of the bin.

"Okay," she called, "who wants kibble?"

"Kibble?" Sirocco said, sticking out his tongue. "Dogs sure have strange tastes!"

"Well, Zephyr thought the same thing about horse food," Sumatra reminded him.

"Shhh!" Kona chimed in. "Leanna's about to find our present!"

And that's when, over by the puppies' food bowls, Leanna discovered . . . six puppy-sized collars! They were made from Sumatra's colorful magic halo ribbons.

Dangling from each one was a little oval carved from a piece of wood. Five of the dog tags were blank—awaiting perfect puppy names. But in front of the third bowl—the one meant for Puppy 3—was a tag etched with the name Zephyr.

"Zephyr!" Leanna read with wide eyes. "What a *lovely* name!"

Suddenly, her eyes sparkled.

 76

"It's a very *Wind Dancery* name, too."

Leanna gazed upward, her brown eyes looking just above the very fence where the Wind Dancers were resting!

"She *knows*!" Brisa exclaimed joyfully.

Leanna strode over to Zephyr and tied the pretty dog collar around his silky neck.

"This one's for you, *Zephyr*," Leanna said with a smile. "Now I know who kept you safe and well-loved while you were gone!"

Kona thought she would burst with pride.

"It can't get better than this," she said to her friends. "So, let's go."

"Yay!" Sumatra replied.

Laughing and tossing their manes about, the happy little horses took flight, ready to look for their next adventure.

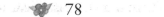

Here's a sneak preview of Wind Dancers Book 10:

Merry-Go-Horses

CHAPTER 1
Drive-by Brisa

One sparkling morning, high above their dandelion meadow, the four colorful Wind Dancers took flight.

Kona, Sirocco, and Sumatra followed Brisa's gaze and gasped. Leanna was indeed tromping toward her family's red pickup truck. Her parents and her little sister, Sara, were with her. And each of them was weighed down with stuff.

Leanna carried an open cardboard box with the biggest, most beautiful tomato Brisa had ever seen.

Sara had two painted model horses in her arms.

The family packed everything in their truck.

"We better get going!" Leanna said to her family as the Wind Dancers hovered invisibly nearby. "My tomato has to be in place for judging before ten!"

"I wonder where they're going?" Sumatra mused.

"Wherever it is, it's too bad for us," Kona said. "I was looking forward to a little Leanna time today. Oh well, what do you horses want to do instead?"

"Wind sprints?" Sirocco proposed.

"What's your vote?" Kona asked Brisa.

When Brisa didn't answer, Kona looked around.

"Brisa? Where did you disappear to?"

"Look!" Sumatra gasped.